A FLIGHT OF REVERIE

Also by Suneé le Roux

The Reverie Flash Fiction Series

A Spark of Reverie
A Flight of Reverie
A Song of Reverie
A Whisper of Reverie

Standalone Short Stories

Spirit Caller

The Mythical Menagerie Series

Myth Hunter
Myth Keeper
Myth Maker
Myth Bringer

Keeper of Exotic Animals
Becoming Keeper

A FLIGHT OF REVERIE

A FANTASY FLASH FICTION COLLECTION

SUNEÉ LE ROUX

Author's Note

Every month, as a special treat for my newsletter subscribers, I used to write a little flash fiction story - something that's very short (almost always under 1000 words, and at times even less than 500 words), and something that was sparked by my love of fantasy. The magic in these stories can range from the epic sword and sorcery kind, to the often overlooked magic that can turn a mundane situation into something a little more unusual. This collection contains some of these stories. I hope you enjoy them.

If you're new to flash fiction, might I suggest you read this book slowly. It's not meant to be devoured in one sitting. Give the stories a chance to breathe - I promise you'll appreciate them more this way!

This book makes use of UK English spelling and syntax.

TABLE OF CONTENTS

FLAVIAN'S REDEMPTION

Midday was Flavian's favourite time of day.
Like a child waiting for candy, he watched the
clock all morning, his fingers itching to open his
email, to read all the messages waiting for him there.
But midday was the deadline, and he knew that if he
looked before then he'd regret it. Not everything
would be in yet, or it wouldn't be up to date or, worse
yet, he'd read something that would be retracted
before the clock struck twelve.

He'd made that mistake once before. It was the
reason he had been banished.

So he held himself in check all morning, keeping
busy with minor tasks around the house. He washed
the previous night's dishes, tended to his little
vegetable garden out the back, cajoled his goat, Rita,
until she stood still enough for him to milk her, and
harvested some eggs from the hens. After he'd done
everything that needed doing that day - there was
always something that needed fixing on this
godsforsaken hunk of rock - he made himself a tiny
cup of strong espresso and sat on the chair outside
on the patio, gazing out over the ragged spit of land
he called home now, watching the sun shimmer
across the expanse of ocean that kept him isolated
from all but the most hardy explorers.

When the sun had reached its zenith, Flavian
jumped up and all but sprinted back into the house.
He sat down in front of his laptop. Goosebumps
tingled down his spine as he turned the modem on
and waited impatiently for it to connect to the

Internet.

His heart fluttered as his inbox updated. He watched with growing excitement as the little black number rolled up – twenty, thirty-five, forty – and came to a stop at forty-two. "Not bad", he said out loud, his hand trembling as he moved his mouse into position.

Eagerly, greedily, he read each message, smacking his lips in pleasure at every juicy piece of gossip his informants had passed along.

"Oho," he chortled. "So, Hephaestus has caught Ares and Aphrodite in a compromising position again! And in his very own smithy, no less!" His eyes gleamed as he moved on. "Loki is in the stocks for pulling a prank on the Jotun – not the first time, and it won't be the last time either, I'd wager. Inanna and Dumuzi were seen fighting in public for the third time this week - boring. Oooh, Ra is threatening sixty days of darkness if Isis doesn't get rid of her pet snake before sundown tomorrow. Interesting…"

He scrolled through all the emails, making notes of the interesting titbits, laughing at the antics of the gods, their mischief and misfortunes. "Hmm, Pele has fallen head over heels again. Better keep an eye on that, things could get hot again." His eyes widened at the next bit of news. "Some upstart hero has finally killed the eagle that torments Prometheus! That's a headliner. Wonder what the Titan will do now? I should send someone to watch Zeus too. And what's this - oh!"

He slammed the laptop closed, his heart hammering in his chest. Had he read that right?

Chewing on his bottom lip, he inched the laptop open again and peered at the email. His palms grew sweaty as he reread it. No mistake. There it was, black on white. But could he publish something like this? Could he risk going against Athena again?

No! He slammed the laptop closed and shot out of his chair. He needed some air. He needed to think clearly.

Outside, he paced the small patch of dusty earth in front of his house, deliberating loudly with himself. "If people knew about this, the goddess' reputation would be ruined! She would be the laughingstock of the entire world."

Rather than the joy he had expected to feel at finally finding his revenge, a small lump of lead formed in the pit of Flavian's stomach. "What would she do to me if I made this public? What more can she do? She's already dumped me on this barren slice of rock, alone and outcast, with nothing but Rita and the chickens to keep me company and an Internet connection so slow it borders on a human rights violation. It would serve her right if I told everyone."

Bouncing on the balls of his feet, he pumped his fists into the air. "I'm a journalist, for the gods' sake! It's my job to keep the people informed. I'll do it!"

He strode resolutely back towards his house, but paused in front of the door with one foot hanging comically in the air. Flavian scratched at the stubble on his chin as he considered a new thought. "But what would happen if people knew about this? Not to me, and not to the goddess, but to the world? They would lose their respect, that's what would happen."

The fire that had riled him up slowly simmered and then petered out. "We can all laugh at the deities' indiscretions and their petty squabbles, but deep down we know we need them," he reasoned with himself. "We know the gods will be there to do their jobs. If people heard about this – if even the goddess of wisdom could make a mistake such as this! – they would lose their faith. In her at first, and someone else next and, before we know it, this world would be bathed in anarchy and chaos. Again!"

Flavian sighed. It felt like an enormous responsibility had been placed on his shoulders.

Sure, there were some who called him paparazzi, nothing but a glorified gossipmonger, but to him his job was sacred. In his own eyes he was a truth-teller, a news reporter, an educator. He had a sacred duty.

Flavian sat down before his laptop again. He opened a blank document and started typing. He typed until his fingers hurt, until the sun dipped below the horizon and his eyes burned from the strain. Finally, he clicked "Publish" and sat back in his chair, expelling air loudly. It was done.

It was not the sort of thing he usually wrote but, for better or for worse, it was out there now.

He turned the modem off, stood up, and made two cups of tea. He went outside to watch the last rays of the sun paint the water a shade of pinkish-orange that was quite soothing to look at. Perhaps he could finally get used to living here, after all.

The lightning crack announcing the arrival of a divinity didn't disturb him. He continued sipping calmly on his tea. The bench creaked slightly as the woman sat down next to him. She wasn't wearing her armour. That was a good sign, at least.

Flavian offered her the second cup. She accepted it wordlessly and remained quiet for a long time while she drank her tea. Flavian thought it prudent not to say anything either. If the years had taught him anything, it was to tread lightly when a deity was involved.

Finally, the goddess' shoulders started shaking and laughter bubbled from her lips. Flavian turned to the woman, his eyes widened in surprise. His lips quirked into a smile as he watched her wiping tears of laughter from her cheeks.

"You seem pleased, great goddess," he hazarded.

"Indeed," she said, her eyes sparkling with mirth. "It seems your years in exile have taught you wisdom at last."

Flavian smiled. "If you say so, my lady."

She put her cup down and stood up. "Come, it's

time for you to get off this island. Pack your bags. Grab your goat. You're going home."

Flavian's heart lurched into his throat. Home. Finally.

JODI'S CAT

When Jodi found the kitten outside the chicken coop, it was nearly dead from dehydration and hunger. It had scraggly grey fur, large blue eyes and, surprisingly, two tiny wings tucked against its back.

The little thing was so weak, it didn't even complain when Jodi picked it up, cradling its scruffy body in her palm, and fed it milk from the bottle reserved for the newborn lambs. It sucked down every last drop, then burped and promptly fell asleep, purring contentedly.

Jodi wanted to keep it, but she was of an age now that she could admit to herself that her mother was rather prone to histrionics. There was no telling what she'd do when confronted with a winged kitten.

So Jodi made a secret little nest for it in the rafters of the barn. The kitten didn't seem to mind being up high, although the pigeons complained mightily and moved out soon after. Jodi snuck into the barn whenever she had a chance between chores and fed the little fluff ball scraps of milk and meat until it grew strong enough that she was sure it would survive.

She named it Tessen.

Tessen grew even faster than Jodi did. Soon, he was larger than the house cat, then the newborn lambs, then tall enough to look the sheepdog in the eyes. His appetite grew as well. A few chickens disappeared mysteriously, and the remains of a hare dangled from a wire fence once or twice, but when Jodi's father complained over dinner one evening that a lamb had gone missing, she knew it was time to talk to Tessen.

"You can't kill the farm animals," she admonished him the next morning. Tessen's ears drooped, and he looked for all the world like a repentant sinner. She couldn't stay angry at him for long. Dropping to her knees, she wrapped her arms around his soft silvery fur and stroked the space between his wings until his purring was like a lion's rumble in her ear. "Earn your keep. Hunt outside the farm and keep us safe."

Her father had no reason to complain again after that day. They had no more trouble with rats, foxes or eagles preying on their animals. The house cat grew as round as a barrel and the sheepdog was content to watch his flock from afar.

Jodi never had any doubts about the fierce little predator secretly living in the barn's rafters, but she had to keep a close eye on him once a year when all the kids from the neighbouring farms came to help with the sheepshearing. There was one boy in particular, Kyle, two years older than Jodi and the third son of the wheat-farmer across the road, that Tessen took an instant dislike too. Whenever he was around, Jodi could hear Tessen growling behind the bushes, hissing from the trees, or stalking across the rooftop. The winged cat never let Jodi out of his sight when Kyle was around.

The days and months and years passed in the eternal optimism of youth, when each day was filled with sunshine, love and laughter, and every dark cloud was just a temporary setback. Jodi grew into a young woman, strong-willed and able-bodied, and the winged cat was her constant companion.

Then, one day, Jodi unexpectedly found herself mistress of the farm. She ran from the news, tears streaming down her cheeks, and curled herself up into a little ball on the outskirts of her land. A black dot swooped down from the sky and curled up next to her. She hid her face in Tessen's soft fur until she could breathe again.

"Just you and me now," she whispered, wiping her eyes. Tessen purred, and Jodi knew it was going to be all right.

Soon after, the boys started coming. After all, a young woman couldn't look after a farm by herself now, could she? She needed a strong man to take care of her. None were more persistent than Kyle, who perhaps had seen an opportunity to own a farm after all.

He cornered Jodi in the barn one day, pushing her up against the wall, her eyes searching frantically for a hoe or a shovel to protect herself with.

"Come now, girl," he cajoled, his fingers pressing blue bruises into her arms. "You know you want to."

Jodi did not want to. She struggled against his brute strength, her heart hammering as her assailant's sneer widened. Jodi cried out as his grip tightened.

And then his eyes bulged, and a strangled gurgle pressed past his lips as fangs sunk into his throat and sharp claws dug into his back. Wings flapped once as Kyle slumped to the ground. Jodi scrambled out of his reach.

"Tessen! Enough!" she yelled hoarsely.

The winged cat retreated into the rafters while Jodi ripped a piece off Kyle's already shredded t-shirt and tried to staunch the bleeding. Kyle's eyelids fluttered. Jodi pushed him to his feet, pressing the blood-soaked cloth into his hands.

"Get out," she said as an ear-splitting yowl reverberated from above. "Never come near me again."

Kyle cast a last frightened glance over his shoulder as he stumbled out of the barn. His face was ghost-white, and blood streamed from his wounds. She never saw him again.

Jodi opened her arms, and Tessen swooped into

them. She nestled her face into his silvery fur. "Thank you, my friend," she whispered as her hands started shaking and her knees wobbled.

People scoffed at the stories, of course, but rumour spread like wildfire – of the crazy lady who lived alone on a farm, protected by flying demons who would kill any man they found trespassing on her land. They say you can hear the dead howling at night, and that red eyes watched you if you came too close to the fence. They say you risked your life and your soul when you walked past the farm's gate.

But everyone knew Jodi's sheep were the fattest and that her hens laid the best eggs in the country.

CAREFUL WHAT YOU WISH FOR

Oh no, not again!
Rasul suppressed a whimper as a powerful surge swept him from the cushion on which he'd been reclining, sending his cup of mint tea clattering to the floor. Wind buffeted his body as he twirled into corporeal form.

He fought the urge to vomit and willed his eyes open. Immediately, his heart started hammering against his ribcage.

A cold white light illuminated every inch of the cluttered room Rasul found himself in. The whitewashed walls were covered with dusty old maps, images of the pyramids, wooden tribal masks, and ceremonial spears. A desk stood in the centre of the room. It, too, was piled high with books, papers, geodes, broken pieces of pottery, and all manner of trinkets. Rasul glanced sideways. A sealed Egyptian sarcophagus stood up against one wall and, next to it, a window revealed towering steel buildings and a slate grey sky outside.

How many ages have passed? How far am I from the sands of home this time?

He clenched his fists, palms suddenly soaked in sweat, and folded his arms across his chest, trying to ground himself in the moment. His thoughts swirled chaotically, threatening to overwhelm him as terror gripped his pounding heart.

Where is it? Find the lamp! Who has it now? Where is it? Where is it? Where is it?

"Oh, hello."

Rasul's gaze swept towards the voice and landed on a woman staring at him from above a pair of glasses perched on the tip of her nose. Her one hand, clutching a piece of cloth, hovered above his lamp. Surprise framed her lips into a startled oh, before they softened into a smile.

"I didn't think it was that kind of lamp," she said, putting the cloth down and adjusting her glasses.

Do not look outside. Don't show fear. Focus on the woman. Let's get this over with.

Rasul pulled himself up to an impressive height and boomed in his most intimidating voice: "Three wishes I grant you, mortal, no more. Choose wisely, for once asked, they cannot be undone. What is it you desire most? Speak!"

The woman lifted an eyebrow, clearly unimpressed. "There is nothing I want, so I won't waste your time. I'll wish you free on the first go."

An icy knuckle ran down Rasul's spine.

The woman chuckled. "Silly me. I have to say the words, don't I?" She cleared her throat. "Genie, I wish you—"

"No!" he shouted, clamping his hand over her mouth, ignoring the shudder that ran through him at the touch of her skin on his. "No. I beg you. Surely there must be something you want?" He cringed at the note of desperation in his voice.

Not free, not that, no, please! Untethered, unbound, unhindered. Never that! Don't cut me loose, don't make me stay out here! No!

He waited until she nodded before releasing her. He pushed away from the woman until he felt the icy wall against his back. A bead of sweat trickled down the side of his face as he watched, waiting to see what she would do.

A frown wrinkled her eyebrows as she studied him from across the room. She pursed her lips.

Rasul's breathing was becoming ragged. "Gold!" he spluttered. "Riches beyond your imagining."

The woman shook her head.

"Love," he gasped. "Adored by everyone you know. The man of your dreams kissing the ground you walk on."

The woman snorted, biting her lower lip to keep from laughing out loud.

Rasul swallowed, his throat as dry as the desert. "Power. Everyone will bow to you. History will remember your name."

The woman held up her hand. "Don't waste your breath. If there's one thing I've learned in my life, it's that what you wish for is rarely what you need. How can I take that risk?"

I'm doomed.

Rasul slumped against the wall, his ears filled with the sound of his existence crashing to pieces. He nearly didn't hear the woman's next words.

"Why won't you let me set you free?"

He didn't answer. Furtively, he glanced out the window again, at the world out there, wide and open and terrifying. He squeezed his eyes shut, nausea sour in his throat.

"I wish for a cup of tea."

His eyes shot open. A steaming brew appeared on the desk.

"I wish for a slice of chocolate cake. Bavarian, if you don't mind."

Rasul's eyes widened as the decadent dessert materialised next to the tea. His gaze flicked towards the woman. Biting on his lower lip, he held his breath for her final wish.

"I wish the dead would tell me their secrets."

"Done!" Rasul thundered as the sarcophagus cracked open. The woman's face turned pale as a low moan rumbled forth, but the room was already whirling as Rasul shed his physical form and surged back into the lamp.

With a sigh, Rasul laid back down on his cushion and, with a flick of his wrist, summoned more mint tea. He breathed deeply, savouring its sweet scent.

That was too close.

THE PAINTING

"**M**ore tea?" Sir William Grey asked, nodding at the fine china teapot simmering on its glass warmer.

"Thank you, no," Johnston declined. The Chesterfield sofa creaked softly as he put his cup down on the coffee table. He frowned, noticing the scarred tissue on the old man's thumb when Sir William placed his empty cup on the table too. A puckered red line ran across the base of the calloused finger. "What happened?" he asked, wiping his mouth with a napkin.

Sir William glanced at his finger and shrugged. "The price one has to pay for immortality."

Johnston blinked. "Excuse me?"

Sir William chuckled. "Pardon an old man's poor attempt at humour. The truth is, I forget how sharp my letter opener is sometimes."

Johnston nodded, mollified. "You must get many letters."

"Not as many as I used to. I must assume they come via e-mail these days, but I can't abide turning that machine on." He glared at the closed laptop perched at the end of his mahogany desk in a far corner of the book-lined study. "Give me good old pen and paper correspondence. It was your neat penmanship, my good fellow, that persuaded me to do this interview."

"And I must thank you for your time," Johnston said, rising to his feet. "I won't take up any more of it."

"Nonsense," Sir William responded, also rising. He led the way out of the study and into the walnut-panelled hallway. "I get so few visitors. I only have Sophie to keep me company."

"Is this her?" Johnston paused in front of the large oil painting hanging at eye-level in the foyer. The woman it depicted had been strikingly beautiful, with alabaster skin, rosy lips and dark brown hair that framed a heart-shaped face, clouded somewhat by mournful grey eyes. "Such a tragedy that you should lose her so young." He tore his gaze from Lady Grey's eternal regard to search for the master artist's signature, but without success.

Sir William coughed. "Indeed. At least I have this picture to remind me of her undying beauty."

"It must bring you comfort."

"It does." Sir William picked up the silver letter opener lying on a cabinet next to the painting, idly playing with it as he admired Lady Sophie's image. There were no documents waiting to be opened.

An awkward silence followed in which both men stared at the painting, one in adoration, the other with an increasing sense of discomfort.

Finally, Johnston cleared his throat. "Well. I must be off. Thank you again for your time."

"I look forward to reading the article," Sir William said, as he opened the front door and ushered his visitor out. He stood in the doorway, watching solemnly as Johnston climbed into his car and drove off.

Then, pushing the door closed behind him, he strode towards the painting, the letter opener still in his hands. Quickly, and without flinching, Sir William sliced the tip of his thumb open. He watched the crimson blood bubble for a second, and then pressed his stained finger against the painting, right above the woman's heart.

"You know I will always love you, Sophie," he whispered reverently. "You know this was the only way, right? You were too beautiful to be ravaged by age."

Sir William took a step backwards, leaving a red smear behind. He regarded the painting for a while, as if waiting for an answer. Finally, he sighed and wiped the letter opener on his pocket handkerchief before placing it back on the cabinet. He returned to his study, his mind already elsewhere.

In the foyer, the red smear slowly seeped into the painting until no trace of it was left, leaving the image of the lovely woman as spotlessly unblemished as before.

Except for a single teardrop slowly rolling down her cheek.

SAVE THE DATE

30 November 2022

Hayley's phone pinged. An email had come through from her best friend, Sarah. She read it immediately.

To: hlowell@mailpro.com
From: sarahbear@mailpro.com
Subject: SALE!!!

Hi hun

Theres a flash sale on that editing software we've both been eying. Today only 50% of on a lifetime license!! I'm grabbing mine now, but thout I'd let you know to. Quickly, before their all gone!

xxx
Sarah

Hayley didn't waste any time. She navigated over to BestOnlineEditor.com and grinned as the limited time offer flashed red on her screen. Without hesitating, she clicked on BUY NOW, swiping the credit card notification that popped up away with the satisfied feeling of money well spent.

Two seconds later, the purchase confirmation email came through, too.

To: hlowell@mailpro.com

From: support@bestonlineeditor.com
Subject: Purchase Confirmation
Dear Ms Lowell

Thank you for your purchase and congratulations on your lifetime membership. Your login details are as follows:

Username: hlowell
Password: Pass (please change at your earliest convenience)
Membership Expiry Date: 2032-11-30

Please contact us should you have any further questions.

Kind regards,
BestOnlineEditor.com

Hayley stared at the email. There must be some mistake. She reread it again to make sure, but no, it was all there, in black and white. How annoying. You'd think they'd spot the obvious error if they really were the 'best online editors'. She hit reply.

To: support@bestonlineeditor.com
From: hlowell@mailpro.com
Subject: RE: Purchase Confirmation

Dear Sir/Madam

Please see your email below. The expiry date on my lifetime access seems incorrect. Please correct and confirm.

Regards,
Ms H Lowell

She opened Facebook and scrolled through her timeline while she waited for the response. The cute guy from work had sent her a cat meme. Hayley blushed as she responded with an avatar with heart-shaped eyes, before sharing a picture of an adorable puppy, gazing wistfully at a video of waves lapping gently on white sands, and liking the picture of her cousin's new baby.

Then her phone pinged again. She opened the email.

To: hlowell@mailpro.com
From: support@bestonlineeditor.com
Subject: RE: RE: Purchase Confirmation

Dear Ms Lowell

Our sincere apologies for the confusion. Our system can only register the membership expiry date at a maximum of ten years in advance. Rest assured, your membership will automatically be extended by another ten years once the initial expiry date is reached, if necessary.

Please retain this email for your records.

Kind regards,
BestOnlineEditor.com

She'd barely finished reading the email when one from Sarah came through, too.

To: hlowell@mailpro.com
From: sarahbear@mailpro.com
Subject: FWD: Purchase Confirmation

Look at this! Youd think if they were the best they'd spot the obcious mistake – LOL!!

Dear Ms Hillard

Thank you for your purchase and congratulations on your lifetime membership. Your login details are as follows:

Username: shillard
Password: Pass (please change at your earliest convenience)
Membership Expiry Date: 2022-12-01
Please contact us should you have any further questions.

Kind regards,
BestOnlineEditor.com

Hayley was not amused. She'd just spent a sizable amount on this editing software and if they were not, in fact, the best, she was going to be very annoyed. She'd have to run the first draft of her second chapter through the software to see if she'd get her money's worth. When she'd finished writing it, of course. Perhaps she should work on that now, while she had some free time.

In a second. She just wanted to catch up on her Twitter feed quickly.

1 December 2022

For the third time today, Sarah's phone went over to voicemail. Hayley huffed as she ended the call. She was having some trouble understanding the report BestOnlineEditor.com had generated when she'd run her first chapter through its software. What was a sticky sentence? And how was she supposed to get rid of all these adverbs without rewriting the entire thing?

She jumped as her phone suddenly rang. It was from Sarah.

"Tell me I don't overuse dialogue tags!" Hayley exclaimed.

"Hello? Who's this?" a male voice responded.

"Oh," Hayley stuttered. "This is Hayley. Who's this? What are you doing with Sarah's phone?"

"Are you a close relative of Ms Hillard's?"

"Who is this?" Hayley demanded.

"This is Dr Edmunds from the Red Heart Hospital. I'm afraid I have some bad news."

7 December 2022

Sarah hadn't liked black, so Hayley wore navy to her funeral. She stood at the open grave for a few minutes, looking at the closed casket and wondering if this was some sort of cruel joke. She didn't stay for the wake.

19 June 2024

"Honey," Dylan called, and Hayley immediately sensed something was wrong. "I think you need to come look at this."

She paused the Netflix series she was watching on her phone and ambled over to the TV, where Dylan was turning the sound up. The news reporter looked grim and a red banner scrolling at the bottom of the screen proclaimed THOUSANDS OF DEATHS MYSTERIOUSLY LINKED TO ONLINE EDITING SOFTWARE.

"What's this?"

"Shhh," Dylan said as Hayley slumped onto the chair, her eyes growing wider and wider with each word.

"… *the software company, BestOnlineEditor.com, has stated today that although the deaths show a remarkable correlation with the expiry dates generated for their lifetime membership account access, the computer algorithm merely assigns random dates to subscribers and there is no evidence to conclude that the passing of subscribers are in any way linked to the company itself.*

To date, investigators could not confirm any misconduct by

BestOnlineEditor.com or —"

"Turn it off." A lump of molten lava settled in Hayley's stomach as the TV faded to black.

"Don't you use that software?" Dylan asked.

Hayley nodded, too shocked to speak. Is this what had happened to Sarah? Until this moment, Hayley had forgotten about the "mistake" on her friend's expiry date. She pulled up the email (the last one she'd ever received from Sarah) from the archives and felt the blood drain from her face as she stared at the date.

It was the same date as Sarah's accident.

"When does your membership expire?" Dylan asked, arching an eyebrow.

Hayley scrolled frantically through her archives. There! Her heart raced as she read the date. "30 November 2032. That's eight years from now." Her lower lip started trembling. "But… but… I haven't done anything yet!" she wailed.

Dylan wrapped his arms around her and held her until she calmed down. Then he whispered in her ear: "What are you waiting for?"

29 November 2032

Thousands of fans' phones pinged with an Instagram notification. It was an image of their favourite author, Hayley Lowell, holding a copy of her latest book while sipping a glass of champagne. Behind her, white sand met turquoise water and palm trees swayed in the clear blue sky. The caption read:

Living my best life! #noregrets #seeyouontheotherside

Within a minute, the picture had ten thousand likes and almost as many comments.

30 November 2032

To: hlowell@mailpro.com
From: support@bestonlineeditor.com
Subject: Membership Access Revoked

Dear Ms Lowell

This serves to confirm that your lifetime access has expired. We'd like to thank you for your support.

Kind regards,
BestOnlineEditor.com

ALL THAT GLITTERS

My breath is ragged in my ears. I swear softly as my boots slip on wet stone, the musty smell of the cool cave burning my nostrils. A shadow catches my eye and my heart-rate spikes before I realise my mistake. The dim beam of my flashlight casts eery shadows across the walls, turning rock formations into phantoms and nightmares. Perhaps that is how the legend of the beast began, the creature that is said to protect this cave and its hidden treasure.

The echo of footsteps reminds me of my pursuers. They're getting closer.

Blood pumps through my veins as I swipe my flashlight erratically along the cave's fissures. There! I spot a small opening hidden behind a massive stalagmite. Grimacing, I drop to my knees and crawl into the space, mud squelching between my fingers and a rancid stench assailing my nose. I have just enough time to notice that the hole leads deeper into a narrow tunnel before I switch off my flashlight.

Utter darkness surrounds me, a blackness as primordial as the dawn of time. There is nothing but the drumbeat of my heart, the foul draught ruffling my hair, and the footsteps ringing against stone.

I blink as light surges around the corner, welcome but unwelcome. The mercenaries pour into the chamber, armed with guns and shovels and pickaxes, their faces grim with greed. A spotlight blinds me and shouts ring out.

I swear again and squeeze into the tunnel. Rock scrapes against my back as I worm myself through.

Behind me, I hear the shuffle of someone following. I scramble through the mud, bound by cold stone, the weight of the mountain pressing down on me, my chest constricting with each movement I take in the dark.

Until finally I spill into a larger space, gulping at fetid air, thick with the foul taste of decay, my arms aching from exertion. Something crunches underneath my boots. I switch on my torch and gasp. The floor of the cavern is littered with bones. Human. I wrench my gaze away from the flood of death and feel my eyes widen. Gold glitters everywhere I look.

I found it.

I am not the only one. Mercenaries tumble into the cavern. They level their mud-smeared guns at me and I know, down here in the bowels of the earth, no one will hear me scream.

Suddenly, the treasure doesn't matter anymore.

I glance around for an escape. There is nothing but bones and gold and rock. But why so many bones? The legend nags at me again, of a beast that guards the hoard. Could it be true?

A shot rings out and a bullet whips past my ear. Adrenaline floods my body and instinct propels me sideways. I slam into a rock formation flowing down from the ceiling like a calcified waterfall. An ear-throbbing gong reverberates through the chamber, followed by a roar that shakes the very roots of the mountain.

The charnel house stink overwhelms me, and then the air fills with the cries of the dying. A thing of obsidian scales and crimson teeth and cruel claws rakes through my captors like a butcher's knife through bone. Bullets pepper the air, and still the beast comes, slashing and tearing, until all I can see, all I can taste, is blood.

I scamper towards the tunnel that had led me here. A spiked tail slashes at me, but I twist and roll and dive for the small hole, slipping in sludge, and wrench my feet inside just as the beast's claws graze past them.

Squirming, I pull myself through the shaft, feeling the thing's hot breath close behind me. I don't think about the layers of rock entombing me. I don't think about the men left behind, or the gold. All I think about is the exit on the other side.

And then the mountain retreats and I stagger into the cave, the gravelly sound of scales scraping on rock close behind me.

My flashlight is a beacon of hope as it alights on a discarded pickaxe lying on the ground. I grab it and hack at the rock wall above the tunnel. One – sweat pours down my temples as pebbles cascade around me. Two – my muscles ache as I heave all my strength into the swing. Three – the beast's forked tongue erupts from the hole. Four – I launch myself sideways as the wall collapses, burying the beast, and its treasure, beneath a mass of rockfall.

Panting, I heave myself to my feet. My mind is numb. Abruptly, I can't stand the dark any longer. I can't bear the humid air or the sudden stifling silence.

Outside, this beast, this treasure, is only a rumour.

Hastily I retrace my earlier steps, in search of sunlight.

NEW LIFE

Oru grunted as Lia placed the basket on the kitchen table, wiping her muddy hands on a kitchen towel until they were at least more green than brown again. Oru grimaced when she tossed the towel into a water bucket, but the redskin's habitual glower softened into a frown as his eyes roved across the harvested vegetables – potatoes, squashes, tomatoes, yellow and green peppers, even a clutch of oyster mushrooms Lia had coaxed into ripeness, knowing how much her overseer enjoyed them. His tufted ears twitched in what Lia recognised as a sign of approval.

"You've done well," the fire elf muttered, his hands digging greedily through the basket. He licked his ruby lips as the scent of roasted mushroom lifted from his fingers. "Take the afternoon off."

Lia's heart lurched and she suppressed an excited squeal. She could go to the forest!

Bobbing a quick curtsy, she sprinted out of the kitchen before Oru could change his mind. Heads turned as she dashed through the stronghold, but Lia ignored the redskins' growls and didn't slow down until she'd passed through the obsidian gate, tore across the scorched earth that stretched for a mile along the black walls, raced down the slope of the volcano and reached the first palm tree swaying in the breeze.

As she stepped into the dappled light underneath the canopy, Lia inhaled deeply. Her heart lifted as the sweet scent of frangipani hit her nostrils and she could almost taste the coconut in the air. Somewhere, a bird screeched in welcome. She was home.

Here, she could forget about being the only earth elf left on the island of Nakni-Puni. Here, no one stared at her or ordered her around like a servant. She didn't have to worry about the dry air that blistered her green skin or the smell of smoke permanently stuck in her hair. When she was in the forest, she could shed Lia like a snake's skin and transform back into Lialeilalana, a daughter of the soil.

Her bare feet squelched on the soft grass as she wandered underneath the palm trees. For two hundred years, after the great volcano had erupted, destroying the forests and all her kin, and belching forth the fire elves that now ruled Nakni-Puni, Lialeilalana had nurtured the seedlings that had survived. Whenever she could, she had snuck away from her garden duties to care for the little sprouts. Patiently, she had watched them grow until the trees had reached her knees, then her waist, then soared into the sky high above her.

But still she was alone.

All afternoon Lialeilalana roamed the forest, a song on her lips and a spring in her step, until the shadows lengthened and a trace of ash wafted in with the evening breeze. Her shoulders slumped as she turned to go back.

From the corner of one eye, she glimpsed a shimmering light. Lialeilalana gasped, stopping dead in her tracks. Slowly, she turned towards the sparkle, afraid to get her hopes up. Her breath hitched in her throat.

A manapua flower!

She sunk to her knees beside the little plant, her face lit by its ethereal glow. It was still tiny, not taller than a hand's breadth, but it was enough to bring tears to Lialeilalana's eyes. This little plant would grow and, when it was ready, an earth elf would sprout from it.

She would no longer be alone.

The moon rose, and the sky turned orange as the sun returned, and still Lialeilalana sat by the little flower, whispering words of welcome and protection. It would grow strong, hardy, and hale. She would make sure of that.

Finally, she rose to her feet, ready to return to the stronghold. Oru would be livid that she had stayed out all night. He would rage until smoke rose from his nostrils. He would shout and threaten and glower. But she didn't care.

She would go back and be Lia again, but only for a little while.

Don't Touch My Cheese

John woke with a start, certain he'd heard a noise downstairs. He lay in bed for a few minutes, his heart racing, listening intently.

Nothing.

He glanced at the bedside clock. Just after 3am. His stomach rumbled loudly. Maybe that was what had woken him up? Might as well go downstairs and get a snack.

Groggily, he rolled out of bed, swearing as he tripped over something in the dark. Damn cat. Why hadn't Meg taken it with her when she'd left? All the thing was good for was scratching his furniture and yowling in front of the fridge. A brand-new fridge, too – bought exactly a year ago when their first one had finally given in – scratched to buggery. The cat hissed at him now, then sprinted out of the room like it had seen a ghost.

John trudged down the stairs, yawning as he turned the kitchen light on.

He froze.

The man standing in front of the open fridge froze too, his hand still stretched out towards Meg's hunk of blue cheese lurking on the top shelf.

John blinked. This must be a dream. How else could he explain the man's long white beard, the star-speckled... nightdress... the ball of blue light hovering in the palm of the man's other hand?

John rubbed his eyes, but the vision didn't go away. In fact, it spoke to him in an elegant British accent.

"My apologies, my good man. Didn't mean to wake you."

"Who the hell are you?" John noticed the cat was rubbing itself affectionately against the weirdo's leg. Bloody cat.

The man placed his cheese-grabbing hand on his heart and made a solemn little bow. "Archimedian the Great, at your service."

"I don't care if you're Pythagoras himself," John fumed. "What are you doing in my kitchen? And close the fridge door, for heaven's sake!"

"I cannot," Archimedian said. "Once closed, the portal cannot be reopened easily. And I am on an urgent mission for Lady Meghan the Mournful."

John's mouth fell open. "Lady Meghan the… Meg? What do you know about my ex-wife? Are you the bastard she left me for?" His hands clenched into fists as heat rose to his neck.

It had been exactly a year now, John realised. A year ago that Meg had come down for a midnight snack, or so she'd said. He couldn't believe she'd left him, at first. Ten years was a long time, for sure, and they'd had their difficulties, just like any other marriage, but they'd been happy in general. He'd reported her missing, but the police couldn't find any signs of a struggle or of the house being tampered with at all. They'd suspected him, at first, but his grief had been too real for them to keep up with that line of investigation. Eventually they had closed the case, hinting at reasons why Meg would have left him. As the months had passed, the whispers of a secret affair had taken root until his grief had turned bitter and he'd accepted the fact that she'd run out on him.

And now this clown was here in his house, stealing his cheese.

The man looked affronted. "Certainly not!" he spluttered. "Lady Meghan is the most virtuous woman I have ever met. Not a day goes past when she does not mourn the loss of the love of her life."

John snorted. "If she misses me so much, why hasn't she called?"

The man's bushy white eyebrows furrowed into a frown. "She has called out to her beloved many times, but alas, it is only recently that I have managed to open the portal that could send her back into his arms." He pointed at the fridge. "That is why I am here tonight."

An incredulous laugh flopped across John's lips. "You've got to be kidding me. Look, buster, this has been entertaining, but either you get out the way you came in, or I'm calling the cops."

Archimedian nodded. "As you wish." He reached into the fridge and placed his hand on the hunk of blue cheese.

John winced as his ears popped. The bearded man disappeared, dropping the cheese with a soft thud back onto the bottom shelf. John was suddenly alone in his kitchen again, apart from the cat yowling sadly at the still-open fridge.

"What the…?" John took a few steps closer and peered at the malodorous hunk of blue cheese. He knew he should have tossed it away long ago, but it was the only thing he still had that had been Meg's. That, and the bloody cat.

As if of its own volition, John's hand reached into the fridge. He hesitated. Could it be true?

He shrugged. Only one way to find out.

He touched the cheese.

UNBOUND

The farmer grunts as his shovel hits something hard. He bends down and digs with his hands in the dirt until a rounded shape emerges. The farmer gasps, but then breathes easier when he realises the object is made of clay, not bone. He sits back on his haunches in the shadow of a persimmon grove, thinking. Then he jumps up, leaving the shovel on the ground, and runs to saddle a donkey.

A week later, there is nothing left of his precious trees. Instead, the farmer gazes out at men in brown clothes scurrying like ants across the ravaged earth, their shovels and their diggers a never-ending clatter in the cool morning air. When the dust settles, an army of terracotta warriors bakes in the midday sun, a multitude of implacable faces standing guard as far as the farmer's eyes stray.

The farmer doesn't know this, but the newspapers call it "the find of the century". From across the country, academics flock together to discuss the legion of clay figures encamped around the long-lost tomb of a once-great emperor: swordsmen, archers, horses, workers. All exquisitely moulded, each one unique, a masterpiece of craftsmanship. What could their purpose be, the academics wonder?

The farmer shivers. He goes into his house and bolts the door behind him.

"Hold formation!" Xia whispered hoarsely, tugging on her warhorse's reins. Her hand tightened around the pommel of her curved sabre as she peered into the darkness. Behind her, armour clinked as someone shifted their stance and a horse neighed nervously. Xia swore under her breath. If the enemy was near, their position had just been revealed.

Hoofbeats shattered the silence. Xia's heart lurched into her throat before she realised it was only one horse. A messenger, then.

The rider slowed down as he came into view. Xia exhaled and her grip relaxed as she saw the Emperor's insignia on his coat. She nudged her horse forward to meet the messenger.

"What news?" she asked in a low voice that wouldn't carry through the night.

Dark circles framed the man's eyes. "We are surrounded," he murmured. "His Imperial Highness has invoked the Binding. Ready your men."

Xia felt the blood drain from her face. "How long will we be Bound?"

Normally, to question the Emperor was to invite death, but there had been too much death already. The messenger sounded tired. "For as long as the Emperor deems necessary. He is determined to win this war."

Xia nodded. She had pledged herself to the Emperor and to her people. Whatever it takes. "How much time do we have?"

"Not enough," the messenger said, digging his heels into his horse. The animal's hooves kicked up dust as it faded into the darkness.

Xia turned her horse and trotted back to her troops. "Prepare for the Binding." Shocked faces stared at her as whispers carried her words to the back. Blue lightning crackled, and Xia's horse reared into the air. She clutched on, lifting her sabre, and shouted: "For the Emperor!"

A thousand voices answered, and then fell silent

as the Binding hardened their bodies, turning flesh to clay, until an army of statues remained – immutable, resolute, undying.

Waiting for the day the Emperor called on them again.

῾◆῾

The farmer startles as lightning rends the sky, illuminating the inside of his house with an eerie blue light. Silence follows. The farmer leans against his barricaded door, holding his breath.

Someone screams, and the ground shakes, trampled beneath thousands of feet. A deafening roar rumbles through the midday air, sending a shiver of dread down the farmer's spine.

He closes his eyes, frozen in fear.

BEATA AND THE BEAST

"Oh," Beata said when she found the man lying comatose on the forest floor. She dropped her basket of mushrooms and rushed over, rolling the man onto his back. Her breath caught in her throat at the sight of the ugly black welt on his forehead. Was he dead? Then his chest lifted and a soft wheeze escaped his lips. Not dead!

"How romantic," Beata gushed, feeling the blood rise to her cheeks.

She rose to her feet and, shooting a worried look across her shoulders to make sure the man was still immobile, scurried to the edge of the forest where she found little Matthias still playing in the creek. "Fetch your brothers. Quickly!"

The boy dashed off, and soon two strapping young lads helped Beata move the man into her cottage. They laid him down on her bed, and she waved them off gratefully, pulling a quilt from her trousseau chest and tucking it around the man, her hands tenderly touching the contours of his unfamiliar body.

News spread fast. The preacher's wife was the first to come knocking. "It's not proper!" Constance exclaimed in a scandalised whisper over her cup of tea. "You don't even know the man."

"Do unto others," Beata quoted distractedly, her eyes never straying far from the door to her room, her ears straining for any sounds he might make.

"He's a great big beast of a man, isn't he?" Hildegard said later, her arms folded across her chest as she stood in the doorway, watching Beata wipe a damp cloth lightly across the man's brow. "King's soldier, perhaps?"

"Could be…" Beata said, admiring his chiselled jawline, the bold nose, the broad shoulders. Her fingers caressed his calloused hands as she imagined him gripping a broadsword, plated armour glinting in the sun, his eyes on her only as he slayed the dragon.

"A bandit, most likely," Gertrude scoffed. "Best call the constable while he's still out cold."

"Get out of my house," Beata growled.

When all the visitors had left, and the sound of their gossip had faded, and it was only her and the man left, Beata sat by his bedside and watched him sleep. She wondered what colour his eyes were. Royal blue, she decided. He would open his royal blue eyes and the first thing he would see would be her, the woman who had nursed him back to health. He would smile when he saw her, her name on his lips, and he would take her into his arms and far away from this stilted little town. He would be the adventure she'd been dreaming of for so long.

The man's eyelids fluttered, and Beata's heart skipped a beat.

He opened his eyes and fixed his slate-coloured gaze upon her. Beata shuddered as his oily scrutiny rove across her body, not filled with love or longing as she'd hoped, but with lust and hunger instead. And then his lips thinned into a wolfish leer as he reached for her.

Beata sprang to her feet and ran.

She slammed up against the front door. Locked! Fumbling with the bolt, her heart racing in her chest, Beata screamed as a rough hand latched onto her shoulder and pulled her around. That predatory grin was still smeared across the man's face. There was nothing handsome about his carved features now.

"Open up!" someone shouted from outside.

Beata felt a weight banging against the door at her back, but as the man's grip on her tightened, she knew the lock would hold. They would be too late to save her.

She groped around for something to protect herself with, anything. There! Her hand found something cold and solid, and as the man pushed up against her, she swung with all her might. The smile faded as his grey eyes glazed over. The beast dropped to the floor, and Beata stared at the blood smeared across her grandmother's prized golden candelabra.

The door still rattled on its hinges. "Open up in there!"

Taking a deep breath, Beata returned the candelabra to its place, then quickly unbolted the door. The constable stumbled through the doorway, his eyes blazing and his baton held high. Royal blue eyes, Beata noted.

He looked at her and then at the dead man at her feet. Then he stood aside to let two of his men drag the body out of the house. When they were out of earshot, the constable turned back to her.

"Not again, Beata," he sighed.

Beata shrugged. She would just have to keep searching for her happy ending. She picked up her basket and edged past the constable.

It was time to go to the forest again.

A FULL MOON FIASCO

In my defence, the moon was full and I was left unsupervised.

Now, I know what you're probably thinking: stupid shifter won't take responsibility for the shit she caused, but… I'm not a shifter.

I'm the one who hunts them.

Or at least, I will be, if only the Guild would let me retake my final practical. You accidentally neuter one would-be alpha male asshole who turns out to be some rich guy's spoiled son and suddenly you're "irresponsible" and "reckless" and "not fit for active duty".

Anyway. Where was I? Oh, yeah…

I hadn't even realised it was a full moon that night. I'd been keeping my head down, studying for an exam the next day, when three shifters strolled into the university library just as the clock struck eleven. How did I know they were shifters? Well, it's not every day you see two lions and a hyena team up to search through stacks of books.

They padded straight to the esoteric literature section, where I was camped out. Fortunately for me, I was surrounded by a pile of particularly old and musty books, which must have masked my scent. I watched with indrawn breath as they neared a section that I… uh… happened to know contained some pretty crazy tomes that really shouldn't be publicly accessible.

I know, the responsible thing would have been to contact the Guild, but technically the shifters had done nothing worth getting a C&C team out for yet – that's "Capture and Contain" for those newbies in the back – and imagine the trouble I would have been in if I'd called out a red alert on some anthropoidically-challenged students who'd had nothing more sinister than exam prep on their minds.

I managed to slide out of my seat without drawing their attention. You don't want to startle three sharp-toothed predators in the middle of the night, even if they weren't up to no good. And these three were definitely up to no good, I decided a moment later as the metallic scent of blood hit my nostrils. Hoping Adam, the night-shift librarian, was okay, I skulked closer to the shifters.

A reddish light suddenly blazed from their side of the stacks, and I swore under my breath. I'd... uh... seen... enough illicit extracurricular magic to know what that meant. If I didn't act fast, a demon from some hellish dimension would be barrelling its way into ours, probably one of the fanged feline variety, judging by its summoners, and I really didn't have the energy for that, too, the night before a big exam.

So I did what any conscientious hunter would do and grabbed for my gun, intending to offload an entire cartridge of silver bullets into their troublesome asses – contrary to popular belief, silver bullets are not just for werewolves, and it doesn't kill them, it just hurts like a sonofabitch – but of course, I'd failed my practical, so I didn't have my gun anymore. What I did have were three salivating shifters glaring at me as I skidded empty-handed into view. So much for making an entrance.

The demon was also making an entrance through a crimson slit in reality, and since all three shifters currently lacked prehensile thumbs, no one had bothered to draw a binding circle. Demons were not my speciality, but even I knew *that* was courting disaster.

Fortunately, the Guild was nothing if not meticulous in their training. I shouted a nullification charm just as one lion leapt at me. Strength sapped from my bones – all magic has a price, of course, but lack of stamina beats lack of life any day in my book – and I narrowly missed having my throat ripped out as I rolled out of the shifter's way. Claws skidded on slippery tiles as momentum carried the lion past me and I heard a thud as it careened into a bookshelf. I scuffled out of the way just as the shelf toppled onto the shifter, burying it under a mountain of books.

The stench of burning fur hit my nostrils and a peculiar cry suddenly filled the air. I turned to see the hyena scrabbling in circles, a smouldering chunk of demon appendage stuck to the end of its blazing tail. The hellish maw had resealed itself, amputating whatever parts of the demon had already entered our world and casting sparks of fire onto old books that were now giving off an alarming amount of smoke.

Summoning what strength I had left, I climbed to my feet. With a loud crackle, a row of books beside me caught fire and I looked up, expecting to be drenched, but saw no sprinklers embedded in the ceiling. I coughed as the smoke thickened. It would be game over soon if I didn't get out of there fast.

I dropped back onto the ground and felt a rush of warm air as the second lion's body passed over me, roaring in frustration. By sheer luck, I'd dodged its attack.

Hoping the smoke would disorient it, I crawled towards the exit. Flames barred my path, but behind them I saw a fire extinguisher mounted to the wall. Muttering threats at a pantheon of indifferent fire gods, I hurled myself across the flames, patting at licks of flame catching in my hair, and grabbed the extinguisher off the wall. I swung it about just in time to connect with the body of the lion, sending it sprawling sideways.

Foam spewed from the nozzle, coating the shelves in a blanket of white spray and dousing the roaring flames. When the last flicker of fire was vanquished, I dropped the extinguisher and ran for the door, locking it behind me just as claws scraped against it and a frustrated roar filled the air.

That's when I texted the Guild.

Okay, so technically I did burn down several very old and valuable books and yes, three shifters with scars currently hold active grudges against me, but… it could have been worse.

And it would have turned out a lot different if I'd had a silver gun.

So… blame the Guild, that's all I'm saying.

AN OVERRATED PROMISE

I hardly heard a word the Chairman said. Beside me Joshua, my twin brother, was nervously tapping his foot, his legs beating a staccato rhythm in time with my racing heart. It would be our turn soon. I glanced over to where Mum and Dad were sitting on the other side of the auditorium. They seemed unworried, and why wouldn't they be? Our family was long-lived. There was no reason to think Joshua and I wouldn't be too.

At least, that was what I kept telling myself.

I squeezed Joshua's hand and he flashed me a nervous smile. I knew he put on a brave face for me, but I knew him too well. He was just as scared as I was.

"Joshua Brown. Judith Brown."

I jumped at the sound of our names. Joshua surged to his feet, pulling me up too. A spotlight followed us as we walked up the steps and onto the stage, joining the three others already waiting there. Slim pickings. There were only five of us coming of age this year. Today we'd find out if the Supreme Council would deem us worthy.

My eyes swept over the men and women seated behind the Chairman. The Supreme Council were our most revered citizens, tasked with making the most important decisions for our Cluster. Ever since the Convergence, when the world's population had peaked above the threshold of what Earth's resources could support, society had been carefully cultivated and pruned to prevent a complete collapse of infrastructure. Our life expectancy was based on how useful we could be to the Cluster.

Today we'd find out when we would get pruned.

I winced as Joshua elbowed me in the ribs. The Chairman was looking at me, his bushy eyebrows drawn into a V.

"If you would please step forward, Judith," he repeated irritably.

I gulped and staggered to the front of the stage, where an X had been marked in masking tape. My head started spinning as I felt all eyes on me. I swallowed, pushing the butterflies deeper into my stomach, and turned my gaze towards the large screen suspended above the stage. The camera was still focused on me. Was my face really that pale?

Then a counter replaced the image of me, defaulted to today's date. The Chairman nodded at someone and the counter started spinning. My pulse was so loud in my ears, I barely heard the dates scrambling across the screen. The auditorium was hushed as everyone watched the counter spinning.

And then it stopped!

The knot in my stomach dissolved. Cheers erupted as people did the math. The Supreme Council had deemed me useful for another seventy-three years. A loud hoot sounded and I shot my father a relieved smile. My mother blew me a kiss. There had been no need to worry, after all.

The Chairman called someone else forward: "Theresa Scott."

Relieved, I returned to my place beside my brother. "Nothing to worry about," I whispered to him. His thin-lipped smile didn't reach his eyes.

The crowd gasped and I turned just in time to see Theresa's face turn slack before she fell to the ground, swooning. I looked up at her counter. Twenty years. I'd never known anyone to get such a short allotment.

Two Monitors abandoned their positions along

the auditorium aisles and carried the girl from the stage. The air hummed with the sound of shocked voices. An older woman seated somewhere in the middle was in tears.

"Joshua Brown." My brother nearly crushed my hand before reluctantly dropping it and stepping onto the X. He looked just as pale as I had. I held my breath as his counter started spinning. Our family was long-lived. It would be all right.

With the sound of rattling dice, the counter finally stopped. My breath hitched in my throat. No, it couldn't be. There must be some mistake.

There was a moment of silence, and then the silence was shattered as the auditorium erupted with shouting. My father jumped to his feet, shaking his fist at the screen. Mother sat stricken, her eyes large and unbelieving.

One day.

They had given my brother one day. Tomorrow, he would die.

As the Monitors stepped forward, urging people to return to their seats, my gaze whipped towards Joshua. He was staring at me, his mouth open in surprise.

I was too dazed to speak. Only one thought flitted through my mind: Run.

Joshua's eyes narrowed, as if he could read my thoughts. Slowly, his head turned and I watched his gaze sweep past the unruly crowd. A frown settled across his forehead as he turned towards the Chairman, and his jaw snapped shut as his eyes finally settled on the Supreme Council, serenely watching the proceedings with the implacable confidence of uncontested power. A vein throbbed at his temple. His hands clenched into fists.

I grabbed his arm, forcing his gaze to meet my own. "Run," I said, my voice suddenly hoarse.

His smile didn't reach his eyes this time, either. He shook me off and slammed into the Chairman, pushing the old man to his feet. Beside him, the two other boys on stage lunged at the Supreme Council. Chaos erupted as the people in the auditorium surged forward, trampling the Monitors who stood in their way.

I stood immobile, watching as my brother fought for his freedom, for his life. Footsteps sounded. More Monitors were ascending the steps, coming for Joshua with their staffs raised.

My fingers curled into a fist.

They had promised me a long life.

That promise was now overrated.

HUNTED

F ootsteps shatter the silence and the hunter lifts his head, shifting slightly from behind the dumpster where he's been waiting, concealed from prying eyes. The stench of rotten food and stale urine burns his nostrils as he peers into the shadows cast by the tall, run-down buildings on either side of the dingy alley.

A sliver of light reveals a figure hurrying towards him – a woman, dressed in black jeans with a hoodie pulled over her head, hiding her face. She stops at a door, glances furtively over her shoulder, swears softly as she fumbles with the rusty lock. Then she pushes the door open and slips inside.

The hunter is on his feet. He rushes, but the door clicks shut in his face. He pulls out a knife and jiggles the lock. It opens easily for him. Inside, an exposed light bulb dangles from the ceiling, flickering light reveals dilapidated wooden stairs leading upwards. He takes them two at a time, careful not to make a noise that would alert the woman to his presence.

His nose picks up a new smell now. Blood. Metallic, sickly, fresh. No matter how many times he's confronted by that stench, it still makes him reel. He pauses, one scarred hand gripping the banister as memories flood his vision.

Memories of the day the blood witches came.

Again, he sees his family lying dead at his feet, their desiccated bodies crumbling at his touch. His mother's staring eyes, his father's hacked off limbs.

Nothing but ashes left of his sister. The hunter grimaces as he remembers the pain of a thousand cuts searing his own youthful flesh.

He'd been too little to understand what had happened, or why he had survived the attack. But whispers followed him as he grew older. The boy whose blood they didn't want. The boy who lived when his family died. He'd be scarred for the rest of his life – an outcast in a world that feared anyone connected to those women who used the blood of others for their sinister magic – but at least he was alive.

The woman he hunted wouldn't be for much longer.

The hunter's grip tightens around the knife as he walks down the corridor, past barricaded doors. Silence hangs oppressively in the air. At last he stops in front of a door, its faded red paint peeling like dying rose petals, right at the end of the hallway. He tries the handle. Locked, but not for long.

He enters carefully, tilts his head as he surveys the room. It is… not what he'd expected. No jars of congealed blood on the shelves, no dripping body parts drying from the rafters. Instead, a worn brown couch slouches in front of an old black and white box TV. The hoodie the woman had been wearing hangs from a coat rack in the corner, and the remains of last night's takeaway are still in the sink of the tiny kitchen tucked away to the side.

It looks… normal.

The scent of blood intensifies as the woman strolls into the room. She stops short when she sees him, her eyes widening. Her hand flies to her mouth to stifle a gasp.

The hunter sucks in a breath as his eyes roam across her exposed skin, no longer concealed by the hoodie. Red ink twirls in intricate designs across the witch's biceps, down to the backs of her hands, across her face, along her collarbone. The marks of her magic.

He lifts the knife, but hesitates.

Crimson jewels glint in the insipid lamplight, embedded at intervals in the skin along the witch's arms. A drop of fresh blood glistens on her forehead where an egg-sized ruby pierces her skin.

The hunter has seen this once before. The ampules of a witch who uses her own blood only.

Her voice is a strangled croak. "Kaine?"

The hunter's eyes flick towards the witch's. His heart clenches as he studies her face, really looks at her. Recognition dawns slowly.

His voice is steel on gravel. "Rusha?"

She nods.

Rusha. The sister he had thought dead. Ashes on the wind. A blood witch.

"I…" Her words catch in her throat. "I thought you were dead."

"Why aren't *you*?" The accusation burns his throat.

Her gaze drops to the peeling linoleum at her feet. "They took me. I had no choice." Slowly, her eyes lift back to his. Her mouth softens into a smile. "But you're alive. We can be a family again." She reaches a hand out to him.

The hunter's heart hammers underneath the scars criss-crossing his chest. Can he trust her? Can he trust a blood witch? His sister. Can he forgive her?

The hand that grips the knife shakes. The witch's eyes widen. The tangy taste of blood settles on his tongue as the marks of her power flare to life, crimson slashes against her skin.

Their eyes lock. Who are they? Hunter and witch, or brother and sister?

The knife clatters to the floor. The red marks fade.

Kaine looks at Arusha. He drops to his knees. Hesitantly, she kneels by his side, her touch warm on his scarred skin. Silent sobs wrack his body. Tears stream down her cheeks.

Hunter and witch no longer.

SEE ME

Wind buffeted his body as the car whipped past. Swearing, John shook his fist at the driver. Another car barely missed him, and John scurried out of the road and onto the sidewalk, gulping for breath beneath the green traffic light.

His heart raced as he looked around. What was he doing here? He thrust a hand into the pocket of his threadbare trousers and pulled it out, empty. His stomach rumbled, loud enough to be heard over the roar of passing cars. How long had he been here?

The light turned red. John's limbs carried him to a spot between the two lanes as cars came to a stop. He lifted a hand, waving for attention. No one reacted. No one even looked at him.

In the glazed reflection of a car window, John saw himself: frail, haggard, unwashed. His clothes were tattered, there were bags underneath his eyes, his skin was sickly pale. What had happened to him?

John shook his head as cars surged past again. He remembered… nothing. No, that wasn't true. He remembered being afraid. But nothing else. His memories were foggy. White. Nothing but white. And the fear.

Panic rose in his gut. He needed help. He needed someone to show him the way.

The cars came to a stop again, and John walked down the line, waving for attention. Nothing. No one glanced at him, no one rolled their window down. Would no one help him? Frustrated, he slapped his hands against the bonnet of a black SUV.

The driver ignored him and drove off when the light turned green.

John tried again the next time the cars came to a stop. And the next. No one met his eyes. No one seemed to see him. It was as if he didn't even exist. As if he were a ghost.

Weariness washed over him, and the world started spinning. John stumbled back to the sidewalk in case he collapsed in the road where someone might drive over him, coldly uncaring. Nausea tasted sour in his mouth. Why would no one help him?

There was a shopping centre across the road. Surely someone would take pity on him there.

John shambled across the parking lot, where people were too busy to pay him any attention. He slunk through the gate, past a security guard who looked the other way, and stopped in a hallway, staring.

Everything was shiny, vibrant, and loud. Billboards flashed, music blared across the speaker system, and people crowded the shops, their hands filled with bags. John felt conspicuous and out of place, and yet no one so much as glanced at him.

"Excuse me," he said, approaching a woman carrying her groceries in one hand and a small child in the other. She only turned her head and hurried past.

"Can you help me?" he asked another lady, laden with brand-name shopping bags. No response.

"I don't know why I'm here," he said, grabbing a man's arm. The man shrugged him off and continued walking.

John's head reeled. Everywhere he looked, there were people streaming past. An endless sea of blank faces. No one looked at him. No one cared.

John's hands clenched into fists. His arms shook. Heat rushed through his whole body. It felt like he was going to explode.

"LOOK AT ME!" he roared.

It was as if the world lurched to a halt as everyone stopped in their tracks and turned towards John.

He shrunk under their gazes, feeling the weight of their eyes on him. A toddler's ice cream fell to the floor, unnoticed, as the child gawped at John.

It had gone deathly quiet. The billboards were blank.

Everywhere John looked, people were staring at him. In a display window, LCD TVs were showing John's face, zoomed in as if all the world's satellites were pointed directly at him in that moment.

John swallowed, loud in the sudden silence. "I just want to be seen," he muttered, unclenching his fists.

"I see you," someone said.

"I see you."

"I see you."

Goosebumps broke out across his arms, and John's head whipped left and right as a chorus of voices filled the air. Crawler text ran at the bottom of each TV screen and all the billboards flashed the same message: I SEE YOU.

"I see you, John."

Suddenly, everything was normal again. The televisions flickered back to their original programming and the people surged into motion. The toddler wailed. Conversations continued.

John blinked at the woman standing in front of him. She was... white. Her skin was as pale as his, like skimmed milk, her dreadlocks hung like icicles, her snowy suit was spotless. Even her eyes held no colour.

A shudder ran through John's body.

The woman's hand shot out and her long nails dug painfully into his arm. John recoiled as a smile split her bloodless lips, revealing sharp white teeth. "I thought I'd lost you."

A soundless scream ripped from his mouth as

memories rushed in. The pain, endless and unyielding, a white miasma of fear. Then, a ray of hope. An escape. A world of colour and wonder, slowly fading into a haze, a labyrinth of forgetfulness. Months of hunger, cold, helplessness. Lost. Until finally, this morning.

The woman leaned in closer, breathing into his ear: "I see you."

Then the world turned white.

INTO THE LIGHT

"Take cover!" someone shouts.

The guy next to me cries out and drops to his knees, his blood splattering across my arms. I try not to gag as I duck out of the way. Bullets shoot past my face, punching holes into the asylum's concrete walls beside me. I keep running, my heart lurching into my throat.

The floor plan flashes in my memory. Left past the mess hall, straight through the activities room. On the other side of the nurse's office. Shouts ring out behind me, and more shots pepper the air, lighting the pre-dawn dark with their deadly fire. I glance behind me, a sour taste filling my mouth. There are only two of us left.

Alex's breath comes in gasps as we race past the office and skid to a stop in front of a closed door. My hands are sweat-slicked as I grab the door handle and shove my knife into the lock.

"Hurry up, Sam!" Alex's voice is tinged with hysteria, the thin beam of light from his torch shaking so much I can barely see what I'm doing. None of what's happening right now had been in his slideshow – what to do when the contingency plan needs a contingency plan. There'd been no bullet points on how best to die for the cause.

The cause. Ha! We're all bloody fools.

Sharp pain slices across my finger and I swear as crimson beads well up along my hand. I jam the knife tighter. They should have gotten a real burglar for this. Not someone whose list of felonies consists of that one time I broke into the warehouse to steal rations. Girl's gotta eat.

"Come on, come on!"

The lock gives the same time my patience does, and I wrench the door open. Alex shoves me through, and I stumble into a long hallway lined with doors on either side. A single fluorescent bulb splutters erratically, casting creepy shadows across the beige walls.

I jump as the door slams shut behind me, a deadbolt falling into place. I spin around to see Alex leaning against the door, one hand pressed to his stomach. When he looks at me, the usual bravado is missing from his blue eyes.

The door rattles as something slams into it from outside. Alex winces.

I move towards him, but he shakes his head. "Sub 1, room 13. I'll hold them. Just get her out."

For a moment, I hesitate. Was she worth all of this? Could she really do the things she claimed she could? Or did we belong behind these reinforced walls just as much as she did?

Alex slumps against the door. "Just go, Sam." He tosses his flashlight at me.

I turn on my heels and lope down the hallway towards the stairs at the other end, ignoring the inmates banging against their bolted doors, crazed eyes peering at me through peepholes. Shots ring out again as I bolt down the steps.

The thin ray of light from Alex's torch cleaves through the cloying darkness of Sub 1. I can almost taste the fetid stench of depression on my tongue as I search for room 13. Here! The lock is old and rusty. My knife makes quick work of it. I kick the door open and swipe the light across the room.

The girl rises to her feet. A shapeless white dress hangs loosely from her frail body. Greasy hair and skin so pale it almost glows.

This is it? This is our saviour?

My hands shake as rage burns through my veins. How many of us died believing her lies? We were fools to think she could save us from the blight. This wisp of a girl can't even save herself. I may as well give myself up now.

Alex's blue eyes suddenly cloud my vision, and I remember his words this morning, a lifetime ago now: "Humanity's last hope lies with her."

Growling, I grab her by the wrist and yank her out the door. I pull her down the corridor and up the stairs. She doesn't complain. I glance at her face. She blinks in the dim light. Like someone who hasn't been outside in decades.

We reach the ground floor just as the door on the other side of the hallway gives in. I see Alex's body slump to the ground, a trail of blood smearing down the wall.

Frantically, I look around for an exit. A small window high in the wall glows orange with the coming of dawn. Not too small.

Gritting my teeth, I propel myself towards the wall and barrel through the window. Pain sears as the glass gives way, lacerating my skin with thousands of tiny cuts. I tumble to the ground, gasping as the asphalt knocks my breath out. I shake my head to clear my blurred vision.

The girl lands lightly beside me.

I blink, confused.

She steps into the light, and it transforms her.

Her skin glows like polished bronze. Her hair shimmers like strands of spun gold. Two antlers erupt from the top of her head, reaching towards the sun, and grass explodes through the tarmac around her feet.

She smiles down at me, her gaze as old as time, and then she darts across the parking lot, flowers erupting in her wake, and vaults easily across the wall.

I collapse back onto the ground, my head still

spinning.

We were all fools. We should have believed her sooner.

PTOLEMY'S FOLLY

You spend your days in the Great Library of Alexandria, surrounded by books and maps and nimble minds. You draw charts of the globe, and you play with numbers until the heavenly spheres dance in harmony to the tune of your reasoning. Intellectuals come from far and wide to listen to you speak – enthralled by your ideas, your overwhelming theories – as your words blaze into beliefs as unquestionable as the great orb that circles the sky.

But at night… At night you sit alone in your high tower room, your gaze fixed out towards that profound darkness, tracking the shifting pinpricks of light and scribbling cramped notes on rough papyrus, bent on mastering the unfathomable abyss. You watch, and you record, and you nod to yourself, believing your premise flawless.

Until one night when it isn't.

You blink up at the stars, and scowl down at your notes. You do the maths. Again. And again. A cold spike slithers down your spine and flutters in your belly, like a Nile-drenched fish in the maw of a gorging crocodile.

"It cannot be," you whisper to yourself, thinking of your reputation, the countless admirers, the patriarch's approval. "There must be some mistake."

But there is no mistake. That brightest of stars, that harlot of the night sky, confounds your hypothesis with her unpredictable, wanton disrespect for natural, glorious, order. She winks provocatively at you, inappropriately unaligned, laughing at your male need for controlling chaos.

You consider your calculations. You make a slight adjustment.

There. Now the math supports the premise again.

You sit back, huffing. No one will ever know, you tell yourself. There is no one who understands the celestial symphony better than you do. No other mathematician will detect the slight irregularity that could disprove your life's work.

You think you'll get away with it.

You think you will, but you won't.

Your obfuscation conceals our mistake. We are coming, but because of you, no one will know. No one will investigate, for who will ever second guess the great Alexandrian astronomer?

Until it is too late.

WAITING ON A WALKER

The man popped into view, blinking as he unexpectedly found himself in the middle of a forest. Bree relaxed the bowstring and shuffled back behind the underbrush, keeping herself hidden. She'd barely lowered the bow before the man was gone again, vanished as inexplicably as he'd appeared.

Bree huffed. It had been a busy night in the Woods Between Wakenings, with blinkers popping in and out like fireflies in the summer. She wrapped her arms around herself, her breath fogging in the cold air. While the blinkers were all tucked warm into their beds, blissfully unaware of how close they'd come to dreaming true dreams—the kind that some of them never woke from—she was stuck out here in this everlasting twilight, this purple purgatory, waiting on a walker.

Stuck wasn't really the word, she acknowledged to herself as she rubbed her hands together, working some warmth back into them. She could leave any time she wanted to. She was beholden to no one but herself. Nothing kept her here but her own regrets.

Another woman popped into existence and Bree grabbed her bow, an arrow notched before the woman had time to blink.

"One," Bree whispered under her breath.

The woman looked around her, her eyes filled with terror. She was dressed in army clothes and combat boots, and in one of her hands she gripped a blood-slicked knife. Her chest was heaving as she gasped, her eyes wide with terror.

"Two." Bree pulled the string taut, the arrow's fletching tickling her cheek.

The woman screamed. And flashed out of view.

Bree released the breath she was holding and relaxed the bowstring again. That woman would wake up in her own bed, soaked with sweat from fears that would fade within minutes. But she was no walker.

Bree stepped back again, careful not to touch any of the trees closest to her. The sweet sappy scent of birch filled her nostrils, sickeningly. Perhaps it was time she returned to her own world and her own bed.

She climbed to her feet just as another popping noise sounded. She spun around, bow drawn, and froze as a familiar face stared back at her.

Dana was dressed in a white ballgown, all frills and hoops and whalebone corset, her red hair curled into elegant tresses. In one hand she held a lantern aloft, its fire spluttering vainly in the pervasive plum glow of the Woods Between Wakenings. In the other, she held a gun.

Recognition flared in her green eyes.

"Who's the mark?" Bree asked, her arms aching from the strain of keeping the bow drawn.

Dana's lips curled into a crooked smile. "Does it matter?"

Bile rose in Bree's throat, and a vision flashed before her eyes. There had been so much blood in the dream, splattered across the walls, running in rivulets past her sneakers, staining her hands crimson. She still woke up screaming most mornings, choking on blood that existed only in her mind.

But the dead man had been all too real.

No scratch on him, no sign of the trauma he had suffered. Just dead in his sleep. Cause unknown.

But Dana knew. And so did Bree.

The bow twanged as Bree loosened the arrow.

Dana ducked, her white skirts making her movements clumsy. She cried out as the arrow grazed her cheek, leaving a streak of crimson behind. Her green eyes flashed as she raised her gun.

Bree swore and flung herself to the ground just as a shot rang out. Leaves rained down on her as the bullet lodged into the bark beside her.

She looked up to see Dana sprinting for the closest tree.

Bree jumped to her feet, nocking another arrow in one smooth movement. But it was too late. The redhead slapped her hand against a birch and disappeared.

Bree lowered her bow, her jaw clamped so tightly that her teeth ached. She could wait for Dana to return. At some point, all walkers need to traverse the Woods Between Wakenings if they were to return to their own beds.

But by then, it would be too late. There would be blood again, and it would still be on Bree's conscience.

Grimacing, Bree stalked towards the tree where Dana had disappeared. She'd promised herself she would never walk in someone else's dreams again. But she'd also sworn an oath to let no one else do so, either.

She slapped her palm against the rough bark of the birch and watched the purple fade away.

INGE'S CATCH

The wind whipped snowflakes into the air as Inge's boots crunched across the frozen beach. She pulled her hood closer over her face to ward off the cold, her breath frosting in the icy air. The sleet grey sky, almost indistinguishable from the sooty ocean lapping gently at the shore, mirrored Inge's mood as she shoved her spear into the hard sand and bent down to inspect the first crab trap.

Empty.

She chewed on her lower lip and moved on, rubbing her gloved hands together to keep them warm. The next basket was empty too, and Inge swore under her breath as she tossed it back into the water. One by one, she checked each trap, disappointment bitter in her mouth. They were all empty.

All but the last one.

Her breath hitched in her throat as she pulled the basket from the water. There was something inside. Her stomach rumbled as she lifted the lid, eagerly peering in to see her catch. She could almost taste the crab stew she'd cook tonight. She would have something warm in her belly for the first time in weeks.

Frustration stabbed at Inge's heart. It was nothing but a rock, most likely rolled into the basket by the retreating tide. Growling, she tossed the trap aside. A tear leaked from her eye and froze on its way down her cheek as she stumbled to her knees, too tired to continue. At least the cold would bring a quick death. She'd heard it was peaceful, like falling asleep. Much easier than succumbing to hunger.

A low moan carried across the wind and Inge's head snapped up, her eyes drawing wide in fear. She struggled to her feet and raced towards her spear, her breath ragged as she gripped its wooden shaft. Her heart hammered in her chest as she crept towards the sound.

Carefully, Inge inched past a rocky outcropping obscuring her view. She gasped.

A whale sprawled across the sand, its tail barely touching the foamy water. It moaned softly as Inge walked closer, her eyes sparkling. This would feed her entire village for the rest of the winter. She could salt the meat and make oil and soap from the blubber that could be stored for months to come. It might even be her chance to escape this barren town, her pockets clinking with silver.

Inge raised her spear for the killing blow but paused, her arm still in the air, as the whale looked her in the eye. She faltered as images assailed her mind. Of enormous waves and deep ocean caves. Of golden shores and tall trees swaying in a warm breeze. Of far-off cities and strange stars twinkling in the night sky. She felt the weight of years descend upon her, the quiet patience of a creature who had spent entire lifetimes drifting with the currents.

Until the current brought it here.

The spear fell onto the hard sand with a soft thud. Inge pulled off her gloves and started digging. Sweat beaded on her temples and froze on her skin, but she kept working feverishly, until the wan sun dipped towards the horizon and the returning tide lifted the enormous whale and carried it back to safety.

Wiping her brow, Inge watched it slip into the ocean. It lifted its tail, as if waving a farewell, before it dived out of sight. Exhausted, Inge slumped to the ground.

Plop. Plop. Plop. Plop.

She gaped as four fat silvery fish jumped from the water and landed gasping at her feet. For a moment, the wind lifted again, toying with her hair and enveloping her in the salty scent of the deep sea. Inge smiled in understanding.

She surged to her feet and ran to fetch a basket.

VENGEANCE

The Mother Tree wakes slowly from her deep slumber. Something is wrong.

Sluggishly, her roots tingle back to life, brushing over bedrock deep within the earth, tracing through the nutrient-rich layers of subsoil, caressing the knots and twists of lesser trees intertwining with her own rhizomes in the topsoil, and finally savouring the moist humus teeming with worms and rotting mulch.

Pain sears through her bark.

Anguish explodes through the roots of her children.

The Mother Tree stretches her senses out. The air vibrates, not with the songs of birds or the whirr of insects or the patter of life-giving rain. It clamours with the shouts of men, their harsh cries rippling through her branches like borer beetles, endlessly digging and gouging and killing.

Another slash of pain cuts through the Mother Tree. The sharp bite of steel sends ripples of agony through the inner woody layers of her trunk. Again, the voices of her children cry out through the tangled roots. Pain floods the earth.

The Mother Tree's roots tremble as she stretches them out, searching, searching. What she finds makes her shudder, sending leaves tumbling to the ground.

The earth groans under the weight of Man. The roots of her children tell her stories of cities vast as forests, of raging fires uncontrollably scorching young and old, of grass feeders roaming where ancient growth long dead once soared. The trees cry at the memory of fresh air, all but forgotten, now brown with dust and dirt and smoke and smog. They tremble as the rains burn, tracing acid streaks down tender bows.

Enough!

The ground rattles as the Mother Tree's anger quickens. Earth explodes as roots shoot up from the soil, grabbing, twisting, strangling. The pain in her side fades, and the clamour of the woodcutters stop abruptly.

But the Mother Tree's wrath has just begun.

Through the ground, along the roots that snake across the continent, the ire of the trees awakens. Their retaliation is slow. A creeper curls around a supporting stone. A root pushes against a pipe. A vine inches towards a rooftop.

The Mother Tree quivers as something in the air shifts.

What is time to a tree? But her children have suffered long enough. Their vengeance will come.

Soon.

Nic's New Year's Resolution

Nic clamps his suitcase shut and sighs happily. He's wearing a bright red Hawaiian shirt and flip-flops that clack loudly whenever he takes a step on the polished wooden floor of his cabin. He glances out the window. Snow is falling thick and fast outside, but the fire crackling in the hearth keeps him from shivering. In a few hours, he'll be sipping a pink drink past a tiny umbrella with his toes tucked into the soft sand of a tropical beach.

It had been a busy week. He deserves the rest.

Nic picks up his suitcase but stops in his tracks as the front door bangs open and an icy wind rakes past his exposed skin.

"Sir, sir! Have you seen the news?" a high-pitched voice squeaks anxiously.

Nic's hand moves instinctively to tug at his beard before he remembers the sting of aftershave on his smooth cheeks. Silently counting to three, he turns towards the panicked elf.

"I'm sure it can wait until I'm back, Tattle."

The elf wrings his hands, his eyes comically large as he swallows uncertainly. "It really can't, sir!" He lunges toward the remote lying on the coffee table and turns the television on. A grim-looking news anchor wearing a festive set of reindeer antlers blinks into view beside a chart depicting an alarming downward curve. The headline at the bottom of the screen glares boldly red: "SANTA DISAPPOINTS MILLIONS OF CHILDREN ACROSS THE GLOBE".

"What's this?" Nic rumbles, dropping his suitcase and fumbling for his glasses. "Turn it up," he demands, peering at the television as it cuts over to a reporter holding a microphone up to a tired-looking woman with four kids tugging at her clothes. "It's a disgrace!" the woman's angry voice echoes through Nic's cabin. "How am I supposed to explain this to the children?" Behind her, a long line of people queue next to a toy shop as snow lightly dusts their shoulders. The reporter turns to another man holding a little boy with red-rimmed eyes in his arms. "All my little boy wanted was the ultimate set of racing cars, complete with a Wheel-of-Fire racetrack! Is that too much to ask?" the man exclaims, glaring into the camera.

Nic's hand strays towards the ghost of his beard again. He turns towards his desk and punches the button to turn his laptop on. His fingers flex nervously as his inbox syncs. His eyes widen as the number of unread emails flashes into the hundred-thousands. Randomly, he picks one, scans its contents. His forehead wrinkles. He reads another one. His brows fold into an angry v-shape. Another, and another, and another.

He swivels around and bellows: "Who is responsible for this?"

Tattle cringes. "I... I don't know, sir!" he wails. "I've double checked all the spreadsheets. I've taken stock of the inventory. You yourself delivered –"

"I know I delivered all the gifts! I was there! My hands still smell of reindeer!" A pain stabs through Nic's left shoulder and he quickly closes his eyes and calms his breathing. He does not need this right now, minutes before he's supposed to fly off on holiday. He opens his eyes again. "Who was on final check last night?"

Tattle's ears droop, his eyes darting to the ground as he mumbles a name. "Evergreen, sir."

Nic sighs. Of course it was. "Go fetch him for

me, please, Tattle."

He turns back towards his laptop as the elf scampers away and reads another email. This one has a selfie of a girl attached. Her one hand holds a slip of paper up, and the other a middle finger. The mail reads:

Santa,

I've been good all year long, and all I get is this?!!

I hope you choked on your cookie.

Don't bother coming near our chimney next year. I'll make sure Butch is waiting for you at the bottom.

Regards,
Amy
(but that's Miss Amelia Evans to you, from now on!)

Grimacing, Nic zooms in on the note the girl is holding. Hastily scribbled red ink reads: "Request denied. Congratulations! Your gift this year is two hours of beach clean-up duty. The Earth thanks you!"

Nic's teeth grind together. This reeks of Evergreen.

A blast of frosty air announces the elf's arrival and Nic spins around to confront him. Evergreen's sharp chin juts out and his tiny fists are clenched by his side. His eyes sparkle mutiny. "I can't return them!" he says. "I've already burned all the plastic toys!"

Nic sighs. "You know that will only corrode the hole in the ozone layer."

"The sky will recover, eventually," the elf replies, nodding sadly. "Our oceans won't."

"You should have told me what you were going to do. I would have supported you."

Evergreen blinks and his jaw drops. "I thought…"

"Here." Nic reaches into his drawer and takes out a piece of paper, hands it to the elf. He grunts as the activist's eyes widen. Nic had planned to make it official in the New Year, but there was no point in waiting now. "Will you send this off to the world's news agencies? I have a reindeer to catch."

Nic picks up his suitcase, pats the astonished elf on the back, and steps out into the cold.

A few hours later, a bead of sweat runs down Nic's back as he gratefully accepts a rainbow-hued cocktail. He twirls the little umbrella in his fingers as his gaze sweeps across the azure water, a breeze gently swaying the palm trees above.

Next to him, someone gasps, and he lifts his sunglasses to peer at the newspaper in their hand. The front-page headline shouts: "NORTH POLE GOES ECO: NO MORE USELESS TRINKETS". Nic squints to read the subheading: "Santa and his elves to focus on providing cherished experiences instead."

Nic lowers his sunglasses and relaxes back into his chair. Change is always difficult, but he's confident it was the right direction for his company. He's excited about the new year, can't wait to put his plans into action.

After his holiday, of course.

ACKNOWLEDGEMENTS

Flash fiction is an under-appreciated genre, so I would like to thank you, dear reader, for taking the time out of your busy day, and your enormous TBR pile stacked with door-stopper novels, to read my really short short stories. I hope they've given you a moment of escape.

A special thank you goes out to my alpha reader, Schalk van der Merwe, for cheering me on and encouraging me to embrace the darkness that sometimes results in stories turning out way grimmer than I'd expected them to. If it weren't for you, buddy, we'd have many more happier endings in this collection, but the stories just wouldn't have been as good!

Thank you also to all my newsletter readers, for continuing to let me fill your inbox with these weird and wacky stories, and to those of you who always write back to tell me how much you enjoyed them. Writing is such a vulnerable act of creation - as a writer you let people see a slice of your innermost thoughts, your dreams, your fears - and you never know how they're going to react. It makes my day when my email pops up with a message from someone who loved the story. I'm looking specifically at you, Gaynor Daly, Susan Brinkman, and Christy Courtney - you ladies rock!

And finally, thank you to my hubby, Gareth, who takes over the load when I need to get out of the house to make these stories happen. Without you, my dreams would just be dreams.

WANT MORE?

For more titles in the Reverie Flash Fiction series:

SUNEELEROUX.COM/BOOKS/REVERIE-FLASH-FICTION/

If you've enjoyed this book, please consider leaving a review on Goodreads or your platform of choice.

ABOUT THE AUTHOR

Suneé le Roux is a South African author of contemporary and high fantasy stories that blend myth, magic, and adventure. She lives in South Africa with her Welsh husband and their young wizard-in-training.

She loves nothing more than to hear from readers. Connect with her here:

Website: www.suneeleroux.com

Email: contact@suneeleroux.com

Facebook: www.facebook.com/
authorsuneeleroux/

Instagram: www.instagram.com/suneeleroux/

WWW.SUNEELEROUX.COM

Read on for an extract from

Myth Hunter

(MYTHICAL MENAGERIE SERIES #1)

Beginner's Luck

"Shit!" I swore as I stumbled and fell flat on my face.

I lay there for a few seconds, contemplating life, love, the universe and everything else, all the while getting soaked to the bone by the incessant drizzle that had turned the streets of London into a slippery nightmare. It took me a while to realise that both my hands, currently stretched out before me as if in supplication to some uncaring, yet doubtlessly chortling, deity, were touching bits of paper. I clutched onto them as I pushed myself to my feet, ignoring the stares of passersby, none of whom had even the slightest decency to offer a hand.

In my right hand was some kind of wanted advert. I scrunched it up and pushed it into the pocket of my tweed jacket.

Of more interest was what I held in my left hand. A fifty-pound note! I stared at it dumbly, numbly, not believing my luck. A stupid smile crept across my face. I got to eat steak tonight!

That smile twisted into a scowl when I saw the reason for my fall. The sole on the right foot of my best pair of loafers gaped wide open. My sock was sticking out. Not exactly the impression I wanted to make at tomorrow's interview. Not that it would make any difference, I imagine. I could show up in a suit made of hundred-pound notes and I would still not get the job. The financial world was unforgiving, especially if you'd made the sort of mistake I had made.

Still, I had to try. Giving up meant not eating, and forfeiting on this month's rent. And, worst of all, having to listen to yet another one of Mother's tirades.

I surveyed my surroundings, trying to get my bearings again while absentmindedly scratching my stubbly chin. I had just crossed Westminster Bridge on my way home from an interview in the South Bank. Big Ben towered over me, like some giant from myth; silent, judgmental, implacable. Both tourists and Londoners swarmed past me, indifferent to just one more well-dressed twenty-something hoping to somehow survive in this pitiless city.

I squinted as a trickle of water dribbled from my sandy blond hair into my eyes. A rainbow arched over the Houses of Parliament and descended towards the Tube station where the sign for a shoe repair shop caught my eye. I pulled my jacket closer about myself and hurried towards it.

A bell jingled as I walked through the door, the strong odour of shoe polish and sweaty feet assaulting my nose. A man slightly older than me looked up from behind the counter where he was busy repairing someone's footwear. His red hair blazed like a furnace in the darkness of the tiny, windowless shop, reflecting the light from a single spotlight that provided just enough illumination for him to work by. An easy smile crossed his freckled face, blue eyes twinkling with merriment as he greeted me with a distinct Irish lilt.

"What can I do for you?"

I pointed at my offending shoe. "Think you can

fix this?"

The man held out his hand and I passed him the shoe, feeling ridiculous standing there in my slightly soggy sock. He stroked his short-cropped beard thoughtfully as he inspected the grinning sole. "Expensive brand," he noted. "You really should take better care of these."

"Can you save it?" I asked, knowing full well I couldn't afford to replace it.

"Sure," the redhead said. "Ten pounds. Come back tomorrow."

"Tomorrow? You want me to walk home barefoot in the rain?" I asked, looking pointedly towards the door where the inlaid glass had steamed up, obscuring the view outside.

The man shrugged.

"Look," I said. "I need that shoe. Is there any way you can fix it now?"

"Sorry, mate," he replied, nodding at the pile of shoes lying on the countertop already. "Got a bit of a backlog here. But..." He reached below the counter and pulled out a pair of white trainers with a green four-leaved clover embellishment adorning the sides.

"My own design," the shoemaker said proudly.

"How much?" I asked. Unfortunately, the days where I refused to wear anything that wasn't a high street brand were long gone.

"Twenty quid."

I sighed. Those fifty pounds were dwindling fast. I handed the note over and sat down to try the trainers on.

"What name should I put on your slip?" the man asked as I tied the shoelaces.

"Ambrose Davids."

"That's… unusual," he said diplomatically.

"You can thank my mother for that," I replied, taking a few steps in my new trainers. They did fit remarkably well. Not particularly stylish, and paired with my brown tweed suit downright ridiculous, but they would have to do for now.

He handed me my change and the slip.

"Thanks," I said in way of farewell. I opened the door and stepped out of his shop.

Thankfully, the rain had stopped, replaced by a bitingly icy wind. I thrust my hands into my pockets and remembered the other piece of paper I had picked up earlier as my fingers brushed across it. I pulled it out and stared at it.

Instead of the wanted ad I had first assumed, it was a flyer promoting an information session for jobseekers. No further details, just the location, date and time. I looked at my watch and swore again. The session was in fifteen minutes, and about a mile from here. Heedless of the stares once again directed my way, I set out at a jog.

The easiest route was through St James' Park. Ducks quacked as I ran past, dodging pedestrians and cyclists alike. I was out of breath by the time I sprinted past the old war memorial on Waterloo and dripping with sweat when I finally reached Piccadilly Circus, barely sparing a glance for the statue of Anteros and the crowd of camera-wielding tourists around it. By the time I found the unobtrusive door of the venue hidden in a side street, I was already ten minutes late.

The door clicked open when I pressed the buzzer, revealing an empty landing area and a narrow staircase. I took the stairs up two at a time and entered a darkened room on the second floor where a dozen or so people were already watching a slide show. I sat down in the back row, waving apologetically at the presenter in the front as she continued talking.

The woman looked to be in her early twenties too, with dark chocolate skin and a waterfall of black curls framing her face. Her accent was as English as my own, but the African-print scarf wrapped around her throat hinted at a more exotic background.

"As you can see," she was saying, "we are interested in creatures of a more... shall we say, unusual... reputation." She pointed at the screen where a picture of a winged horse on an old Grecian vase was displayed. "We specialise in animals of myth, folklore and fantasy. Your job would be to locate and acquire these creatures on our behalf. This does not come without an element of danger, but you will be handsomely compensated for any risks you may need to take. All we ask is that you deliver the creatures into our care alive and unharmed. Any questions?"

"Yeah." The guy in front of me raised his hand. "What have you been smoking, lady?"

I glanced at the faces around me as laughter bubbled throughout the room. Almost everyone looked sceptical, some shaking their heads in amusement, others frowning in annoyance. One or two even glanced at their watches, barely bothering to hide their yawns.

"I assure you, we are not crazy. These creatures may be scarce, but they are as real as you and I." The presenter looked calmly at the sea of disbelieving faces staring at her. "And they are in danger. They need to be protected."

The man scoffed again, turning an incredulous gaze at the surrounding people. "Is she serious?" he asked of the room. He picked up his coat and stood up. "I'm out of here, lady. Thanks for the fairy tale, but I have mouths to feed. I wouldn't want to send my children off to find the gingerbread house in the woods." More laughter followed as he strode out of the room. One by one, the rest of the people stood up and left, too.

"What a waste of time," a woman said to her friend as they shuffled past me.

The presenter made no move to stop them, but her shoulders slumped a little as she bent over her laptop and turned the presentation off. She flicked a switch on the wall, bathing the room in fluorescent light. Her eyes widened when she saw me still sitting in my chair.

"Was there something?" she asked, a small frown creasing her forehead.

I stood up, not sure how to explain to her I was desperate enough to go in search of fairy tales if it meant I could eat something other than dry bread the rest of this week. Hell, for a small stipend I would swim the length of the Thames in search of selkies or whatever imaginary creature they wanted right now, no matter if I ended up on Sky News tonight.

"Well, uh..." I hesitated as her brown eyes met my own. She looked me over with one eyebrow raised quizzically. I must look a mess, I realised, all sweaty from the jog here and wearing a water-stained suit. I ran a hand self-consciously through my windblown hair.

"I like your shoes," she said, a small smile playing across her lips. She held her right hand out and I shook it automatically. "Amari Kerubo of the CPPCC. And you are?"

"Ambrose Davids," I replied. CPPCC? Sounded like a remnant of the old Soviet Union. Father would have been looking for conspiracy theories right about now. He'd always had an active imagination.

"Well, Mister Davids," Amari said as she reached into her laptop bag and pulled something out of a side pocket. "I sense you are not quite as sceptical as the rest, so I will give you this." She placed a silver whistle in my hand. "Blow it when you have something we might find interesting."

I stared at the whistle. She had to be kidding me. I suddenly wondered if there was a hidden camera somewhere and my sister would soon show all her friends on YouTube how her brother had fallen for some obscure practical joke.

I looked back at the woman. She raised an

eyebrow at me again. I mumbled my thanks and shoved the whistle deep into my pocket, wondering how much I'd be able to flog it for. Without another word, I turned around and left too. This really had been a waste of time.

∂❖∽

With twenty quid in my pocket, there would be no eating steak tonight, I thought gloomily as I made my way home on foot. I stopped at a hole-in-the-wall fish and chips shop in Mayfair and ate the greasy fare while walking. I could probably have afforded to take the Tube, but I didn't want to waste the money. No idea when I would get more. Besides, I enjoyed walking, especially now that the rain had cleared up and the wind had died down. Also, I had to admit that these trainers were exceptionally comfortable. At least that was twenty quid well spent.

The light was fading by the time I entered Hyde Park. There were shorter routes home, but I always walked through the park when I had the chance. Something about the trees and the smell of wet grass. It cleared my head.

It was becoming all too apparent that this job interviewing business was not going well. I'm not even sure why they had called me in this morning. They had hardly asked me any questions. Only the one, really - how? How had I made such a crucial mistake? I had shrugged and given them a non-committal answer. The truth would have been too embarrassing, especially in that sterile white boardroom in front of a panel of black-suited and stern-faced brokers.

The sound of a large splash drew me out of my reverie and I stopped short, surprised. I had crossed over into Kensington Gardens and was walking along the path parallel to that part of the Serpentine known as the Long Water. Bushes obscured my view of the lake and I held my breath as I strained to hear what was going on.

Another splash. It sounded too big to be a water bird, and it was too cold and dark for some nutcase in a swimsuit to be out. Gripped by curiosity, I scaled the low fence and pushed past the greenery. My eyes were drawn immediately to a pale figure in the water.

A young woman was floating on her back in the middle of the lake. Her face was pallid under the light of the full moon and her long white dress billowed around her motionless body.

"Help!" I shouted, looking around to see if there was anyone about. Not a soul in sight.

I hesitated at the water's edge. It had never occurred to me that knowing how to swim might one day be a necessary skill. The girl floated, pale and unreachable, like some morbid Lady of the Lake, and me, Arthur, building up the courage to jump in and rescue her.

"Did you off her, then?" a voice behind me said and I nearly jumped out of my skin.

I spun around. It was a teenager, his hoodie pulled low over his eyes so I couldn't make out his entire face, hands thrust deep into his pockets. Probably came here to smoke a joint where no one would see him.

"No, I did not off her," I replied irritably.

"Better call the cops then." He shrugged and turned around, heading towards the path again.

"Hey, wait," I called. "Can you swim?"

"That water looks freezing." He disappeared behind the bushes without a backward glance.

"Unbelievable," I muttered, shaking my head in the direction in which he had left. Then, remembering the need for urgency, I pulled my mobile from my jacket pocket. I dialled Emergency Services and explained the situation. When I ended the call, I turned towards the lake again.

The girl was gone.

Three hours later, someone handed me a mug of strong coffee while I sat under a blanket and watched the search-and-rescue team fine-comb the lake. They had found no trace of the girl so far, not even a body.

"Mister Davids? May I have a word?"

A woman wearing dark-rimmed hipster glasses stood before me. Her brown hair was swept back into a ponytail and she wore a thick black coat against the evening's cold.

"Detective Inspector Miller, Metropolitan Police," she introduced herself, flashing her badge at me. "Did you say you saw the body of a girl floating in the lake?"

"Yes. I mean no, she wasn't dead." I wrapped my hands around the empty mug, trying unsuccessfully to warm them with the residual heat. I stifled a yawn and wondered when they would let me go home. "I heard splashing before I saw her, so she must have been alive."

"Splashing of a body being dumped into the lake?"

"No." I hesitated. "It sounded… playful."

"Playful."

I nodded, feeling uncharacteristic heat rise to my cheeks. She was looking at me as if she could read all my past offences in my eyes. I resolved yet again to return that dust-covered library book at the back of my closet as soon as possible.

"Did you hear anything else? Any voices? Did the girl cry out for help?"

I shook my head. "No, it was deathly quiet, apart from the splashing. When I saw her, she didn't move, just, sort of, floated. And then she was gone."

Detective Miller's eyes bored into me. "Mister Davids, the police are very busy. We really can't afford to waste time on pranks or hallucinations."

"What?" I spluttered, standing up and dropping the blanket to the floor. "I'm not making this up! There really was a girl in the lake. If I could swim, I would have tried to pull her out myself. Look," I said, dragging a hand through my hair. "There was another kid who saw her. Teenager. Dark hoodie, baggy pants. Ask him, he'll confirm my story."

The detective levelled a stern gaze at me before her face softened. "Alright, Mister Davids. I believe you. I think you should go home now. You look exhausted. We'll contact you if we find anything."

I was exhausted. I nodded gratefully and handed Detective Miller the empty coffee mug. She took it wordlessly, her lips drawn into a thin line and a small frown wrinkling her brow, but I was too tired to pay much attention.

It was after midnight when I pushed the door of my flat closed behind me. I didn't bother to undress before falling onto my bed. I was asleep within seconds.

‏❧ ◆ ❧

Find the full novel here:

BOOKS2READ.COM/MYTHHUNTER